For Beatrice

This edition published 1989 by Guild Publishing
by arrangement with Simon & Schuster Limited

Text © 1989 H.R.H. The Duchess of York
Illustrations © 1989 Simon & Schuster

Typeset in Stempel Schneidler by Pastiche, London
Printed in Great Britain by Cambus Litho Ltd, East Kilbride
Bound by MacLehose & Partners Ltd, Portsmouth

CN 9363

~ BUDGIE ~
The Little Helicopter

H.R.H. The Duchess of York
Illustrated by John Richardson

GUILD PUBLISHING

LONDON · NEW YORK · SYDNEY · TORONTO

It was a hot, hot day. Budgie, the helicopter, was bored. He looked around the huge hangar but nothing stirred. Oliver, the owl, was fast asleep and even Fergus, the cat, didn't notice the mouse in front of his nose. Budgie turned on his radio but nothing was happening.

Every now and then he cooled himself with a whirr of his rotors.
'Same old faces,' he thought, as he looked around. 'I wish
something exciting would happen.' Budgie always longed
for a bit of adventure.

Yesterday Budgie spent the whole day delivering crate
after crate of clawing lobsters from Mulhearn-on-Sea.
'I may be the littlest helicopter,' he sighed to himself, 'but
I wish I wasn't always given the nasty, little jobs to do.'

How Lionel, the Lynx, laughed when Budgie was forced to have a thorough wash and polish afterwards, because he smelled so fishy. There was nothing Budgie disliked more than a good scrub in the helicopter wash.

Clatter, clatter, clatter, blatter, blatter, clatter.
Budgie looked up and saw Lionel.
'Hurumph!' Lionel cleared his throat. 'Hurumph! Um, this is Budgie,'
he said to a small plane who sparkled and shone.

'He's not usually so clean. Must have been forced to wash.'
Budgie blushed red to the roots of his rotors.
'I'm Pippa,' said the plane. 'I'm new.'
'Hello,' smiled Budgie.

Pippa soared. She looped the loop. *Wheeee.* Flew on her side. *Brrrr.*

Then swooped. *Eoww.* 'Hurrah, hurrah,' shouted Budgie. 'Well done, Pippa!'

Just then there was a loud noise. *Whoop, whoop, whoop*
it went. *Whoop, whoop, whoop.*

'That's the alarm,' said Budgie.
'Control calling Lionel. Control calling Lionel.

Lionel come in please. Emergency, Lionel. Over.'
Budgie clicked on his radio. *Whrrr.* 'Budgie to Control,
Budgie to Control. Lionel's out on a job and won't be
back for hours. Can we help? Over!'

Buffeted and blown, Budgie and Pippa arrived at Stanton. They spotted the school as the rain died away. They didn't know which road the car had taken, so they flew in ever widening circles, keeping fairly low. Then Pippa spied a big, black car in the distance. 'Quick,' she said. 'Let's follow them.'

They followed the car for some time. Eventually it turned along a country lane and headed towards an old barn. When the car stopped, Budgie and Pippa flew straight past pretending that nothing was wrong.

'You keep watch, and I'll go for help,' said Pippa. Silently she sped off.

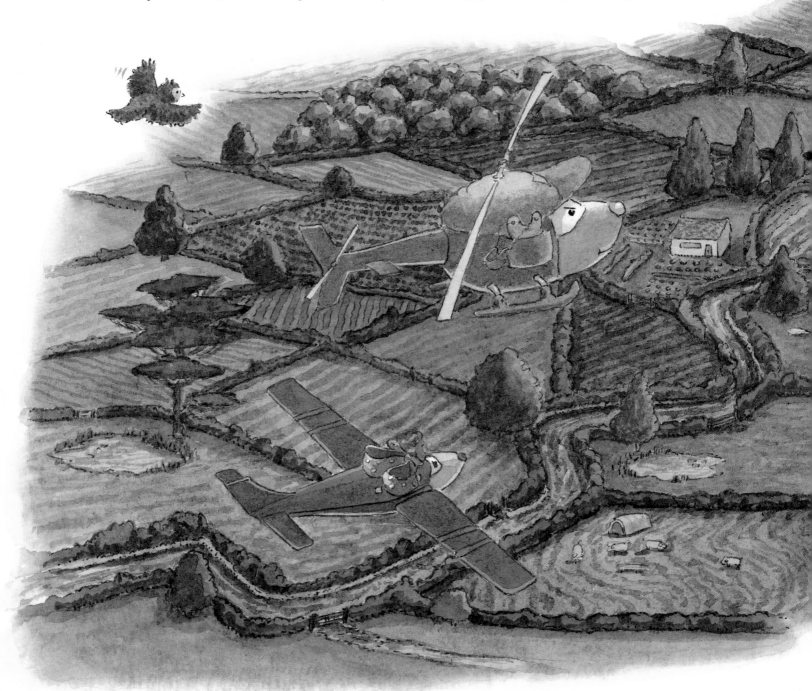

All alone, Budgie flew towards the barn. He turned off his engine
and landed noiselessly. 'Only a light and small helicopter could land
between these trees,' he thought proudly. As he watched and
waited for help to arrive, it began to get dark.

Bang! Crash! There was a loud noise from the barn. Budgie looked
up and heard a shout. 'Get after her.'

'Over here, Rose!' Budgie shouted. 'Look out, behind you. Quick, jump up!'
As quick as a wink Rose was on board and Budgie burst into life.

Minutes later Budgie heard a screech of brakes. The police had
arrived and he heard a familiar clatter. It was Lionel barking orders.
The second kidnapper made a run for it.

'You won't get far,' shouted Budgie.
Then he carefully positioned himself over the roof of the barn.
'Here we go,' he said as he shook his skids.

'Aaargh!' Crash! Bang! Splat!

Budgie landed gently and Rose jumped out. Her parents were waiting, happy and relieved that she was safe, and Rose ran towards them. Lionel looked on, smiling.

'Brave Budgie saved me,' cried Rose.
Budgie smiled. 'What an exciting day it's been, after all,' he sighed,
as he started for home.

Back at the hangar, Budgie received a hero's welcome.
'Bravo Budgie,' said Lionel.
'I couldn't have done it without Pippa,' said Budgie. 'We make a good team.'

'You'd better come with me,' said Pippa mysteriously. 'Now you're
a hero, you'll have to be cleaned up.'
'Oh no,' moaned Budgie. 'It's nice being made a fuss of...

'...but I hate having a bath!'

For Andrew

Typeset in Stempel Schneidler by Pastiche, London
Printed in Great Britain by Cambus Litho Ltd, East Kilbride
Bound by MacLehose & Partners Ltd, Portsmouth

CN 9363

~ BUDGIE ~
At Bendick's Point

H.R.H. The Duchess of York
Illustrated by John Richardson

GUILD PUBLISHING

LONDON · NEW YORK · SYDNEY · TORONTO

Dring, dring went the alarm. At last the day of the air show had arrived. Everyone in the hangar was excited. Everyone, that is, except for Budgie, the little helicopter.

'Not much point in **my** getting up,' he thought. 'I'm going back to sleep.'

But Budgie couldn't get back to sleep. Every time he closed his eyes he saw flocks of sheep. Budgie knew it was naughty to chase animals, but when he was out last week he hadn't been able to stop himself. He had hoped no one would see him. Why did Lionel have to fly by just then?

So now Lionel insisted that Budgie do the parcel deliveries on the day of the air show. Budgie watched Lionel polish his medals and then begin inspecting the planes and helicopters as they came out of the helicopter wash. 'There goes scruffy Budgie,' said Lionel as Budgie passed.

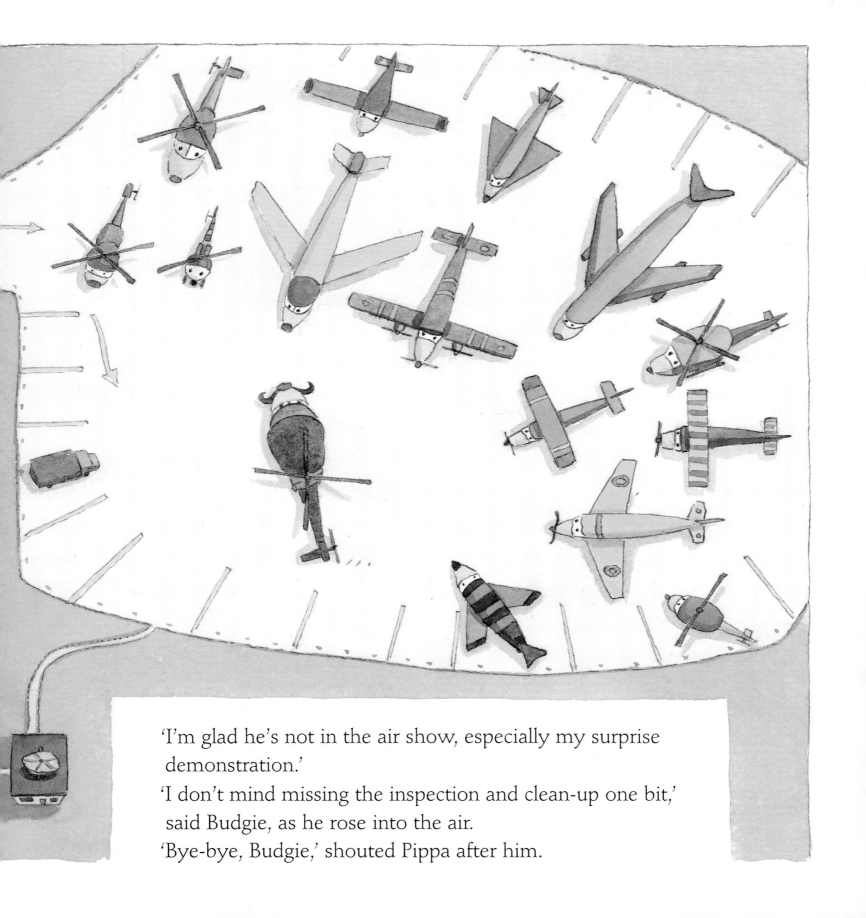

'I'm glad he's not in the air show, especially my surprise demonstration.'
'I don't mind missing the inspection and clean-up one bit,' said Budgie, as he rose into the air.
'Bye-bye, Budgie,' shouted Pippa after him.

As he flew along the coast towards Bendick's Point, Budgie cheered
up. The sea was sparkling and the cold wind whipped his cheeks.
He almost forgot about the air show and what he was missing.

As he looked down, he saw two boys preparing to go out for the
day in their boat. They waved to Budgie as he passed.

As usual, Captain Frobisher was waiting for Budgie when he arrived
at the lighthouse at Bendick's Point.
'Be careful!' shouted the Captain as Budgie lowered the rope. 'There's
a gale warning and the wind is getting stronger every minute.'
It was difficult to hover, but after two or three tries Budgie managed
to unload his parcels.
'I'd better get on with my deliveries,' thought Budgie, 'before the
wind gets any worse. They'll be starting the air show about now.
I wonder how it's going.'

When Budgie returned, the air show was well underway. But watching the display made him feel left out. 'I know,' he thought, 'I'll listen to my radio. *Helicopter Heroes*, my favourite programme, is on.' Just then, Budgie's emergency channel came to life. '*Mayday, mayday. Mayday, mayday.*'

'Hold on,' said Budgie. 'That sounds like Captain Frobisher.'

Budgie listened hard. The message **was** from Bendick's Point. The two boys were in trouble. 'Quick,' said Budgie. 'I'd better raise the alarm. I **do** wish Pippa was here.'

But as he hopped towards the siren, Budgie realised that no one would hear him. The air show was at its exciting climax with Lionel's surprise demonstration. Lionel and Chin-up, the Chinook, were lifting huge weights on a metal cable. It was breathtaking to watch. Budgie tried to attract their attention, but just then, there was a loud crack.

The cable had snapped! It whipped up and hit Lionel's rotors, knocking him into a spin.

'Oh no,' shouted Budgie.

At that moment, Pippa appeared.

The two friends gasped as Lionel made his emergency landing. His rotors were completely bent. The fire engines quickly approached. But Budgie hadn't forgotten

the distress call. He quickly explained to Pippa what had happened. 'Come on,' he said. 'We haven't much time. We'd better go on our own.'

Soon Budgie and Pippa saw the familiar rocky coast and Bendick's Point. The gale was getting worse so Pippa circled high above the storm to keep radio contact with the lighthouse. Budgie flew out to sea and then approached the cliffs. He couldn't see much because

the rain beat so heavily into his eyes. At last he caught sight of the
little boat. The boys were trapped in a narrow cove and the tide
was rising. Never had Budgie seen rocks so sharp.
'Good luck, Budgie,' radioed Pippa.

'Help, help!' Budgie heard the boys cry.
'I'd better lower a rope,' thought Budgie. 'It's our only hope in this
rough sea. Hold on!' he shouted to the boys, but they couldn't hear.

The wind was too strong. All at once a huge, roaring wave hit Budgie's skids and knocked him off balance. Budgie let go of the rope and swerved upwards.

The storm was getting worse. 'I wish I was back at the hangar,' thought Budgie. He looked at Pippa circling above. Budgie knew that a helicopter was stronger in this weather than a small plane. 'It's all up to me,' he thought. He held his breath as he swooped again into the cove. He hovered for a moment and shouted, 'Quick, hang on tight, boys! We're going up.'

Using **all** his strength, Budgie rose to
the top of the cliff. Just as he reached safety,
the boys let go of the skids. People rushed
towards them.

'Thanks, Budgie,' they shouted.
'It's too dangerous to land here, Pippa,' said Budgie.
'Let's go back home before the weather
gets worse.'

On the way back to the hangar, Pippa radioed ahead to tell everyone about Budgie's brave rescue. When the two friends arrived there was a loud cheer. Lionel blushed as he limped forward. 'Er… hurumph,' he cleared his throat.

'Budgie, you and Pippa have both been very brave.' As he
spoke, Lionel presented Budgie with a gleaming medal.
Budgie beamed.
'And now,' said Lionel, 'we've got a surprise for you.'

Budgie had never felt happier than when he led the flypast.

What an exciting end to an exciting day.